What a BRAGGER!

by LeeAnn Mancini

GLM Publishing
P.O. Box 812633
Boca Raton, Florida 33481-2633

GLMPublishing.net
SeaKidsAdventures.com

Manufactured in the USA
Printed by HCI Printing & Publishing, Inc.

Library of Congress Control Number
2015900995

"And now these three remain: faith, hope and love. But the greatest of these is love."
- 1 Corinthians 13:13 (NIV)

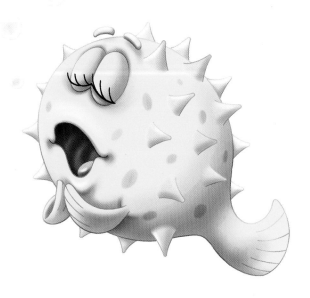

To all my sisters, especially Gloria, Raquel and Criss, who love the Sea Kids as much as I do!

It was a wonderful day at Beneath the Sea Play Park. Melissa was playing in the sandbox with her friends. "I have more sand toys than anyone," she bragged. "I can swing the highest and climb the fastest, and I can blow the biggest air bubble."

"You're fibbing," said Corey. "You can't do all that, and you don't have the most sand toys either."
"Do so," said Melissa.
"Do not," replied Corey.

"I do, and I don't care if you don't believe me.
I'm going home to play with all my cool stuff," bragged Melissa.

The next day at lunch, Melissa shouted, "I have the most delicious ham sandwich! Also, I have the best lunchbox with a picture of Snappy Cat Starfish on it, but I left it at home so it won't get scratched."

"No way! Snappy Cat Starfish?" said Donna.

"Wow! I have been waiting to get that lunchbox forever, but it's always sold out at the store," added Christina.

"Yea, I know. I got mine from a friend who knows Snappy Cat Starfish, and she's going to introduce me to him," bragged Melissa.

100% JUICE

Corey heard what Melissa said and he was angry. After school, he swam home as fast as he could.

"Mom, at the park Melissa said she has more toys than anyone. I know it's not true because she always uses mine. She's just full of blowfish air. Today at school, she told everyone she has a Snappy Cat Starfish lunchbox. I bet she doesn't. She said she was going to meet Snappy Cat Starfish, and I bet she won't. She's always bragging!"

"Why do you think she said all those things?" asked his mother.
Corey frowned. "Probably because she doesn't know how to be nice," he said.
"Perhaps you could help her to be a good friend," said Corey's father.

The next Saturday at Beneath the Sea Play Park, the sea kids were having fun. But Melissa sat alone in the sandbox, crying.

Corey swam over to her. "Hi Melissa."
"Get away from me!" cried Melissa.
"Why?" asked Corey.

"Because I can't swing the highest, I can't climb the fastest, and
I've broken the only sand shovel I have. I don't have a Snappy Cat Starfish lunchbox,
and I'll never get to meet Snappy Cat Starfish." Sobbing, Melissa swam away as fast as she could.

Corey followed her home. What he saw surprised him. The door to Melissa's cave was falling off the hinges. The family dune buggy looked rusty and old, and there were broken toys in the sandbox.

Corey swam home with a sad heart.

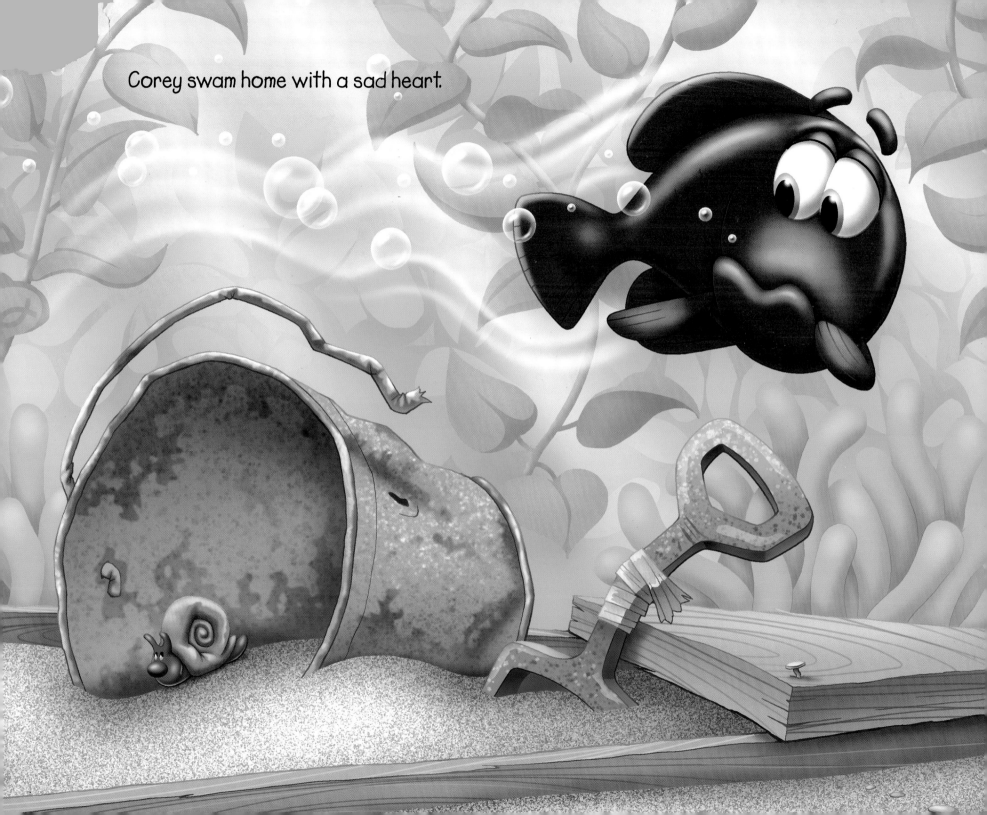

Corey looked around his room and saw all the great stuff he had. His shelves were full of wonderful books to read, and the toy chest was full of toys.

He prayed to Jesus, "Dear Jesus, I thank you for my mommy, daddy and my whole family and all my friends. I thank you for all the wonderful things I have. Please help me to help Melissa because she is special to you, and she is special to me."

His mother called him to the kitchen, "Corey, your teacher, Miss Mermaid, has planned a birthday party for Melissa at school during lunchtime," said his mother.

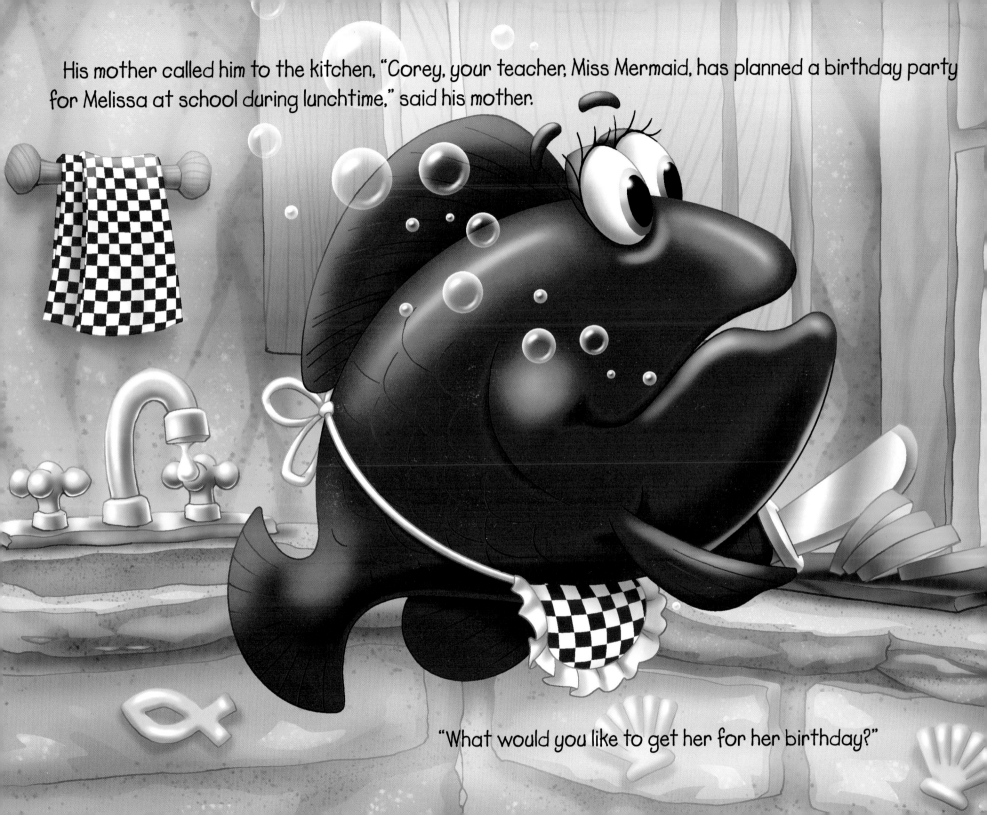

"What would you like to get her for her birthday?"

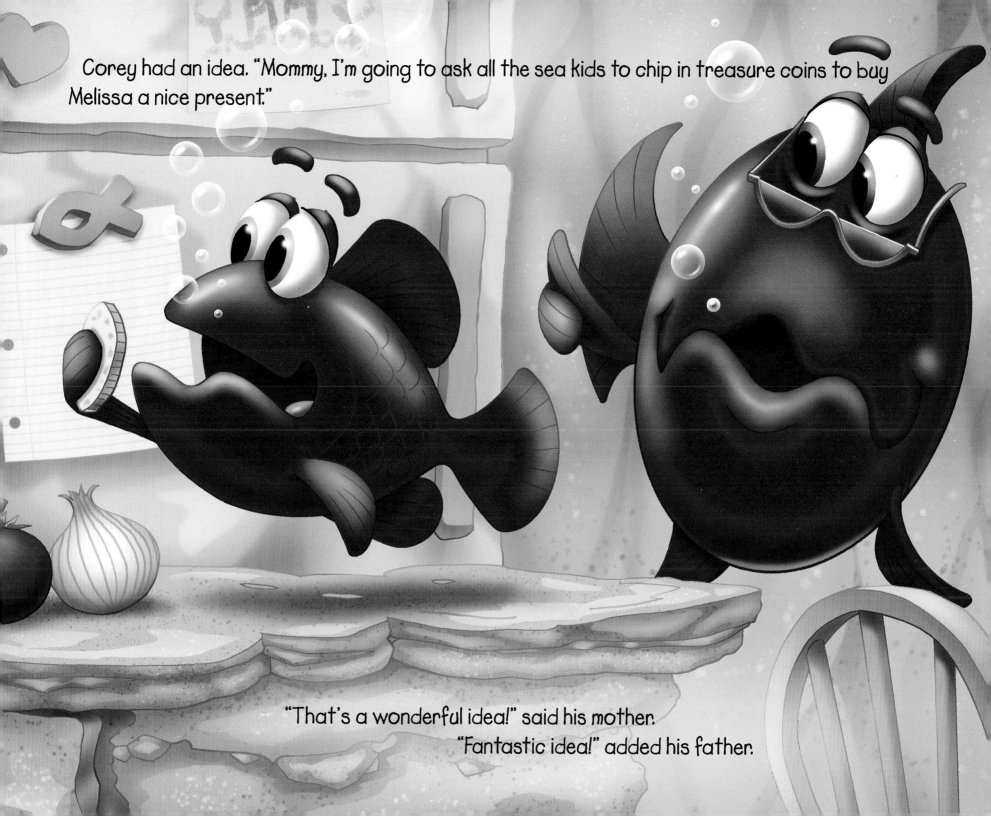

Corey had an idea. "Mommy, I'm going to ask all the sea kids to chip in treasure coins to buy Melissa a nice present."

"That's a wonderful idea!" said his mother.
"Fantastic idea!" added his father.

The next day, Corey and his best friend, Tommy, collected the treasure coins. All the sea kids were happy to chip in their allowances. The grand total was $10.00!

"Let's go to the toy store and get Melissa something really cool," said Corey.
"I love the toy store!" said Tommy.
They swam past all the stores as fast as they could until they reached the Sea Toys Adventures store.

They found a wonderful present, but it was $10.25, and they only had $10.00.

"Mr. Wilbur, can we please buy this present for Melissa Blowfish even if we only have $10.00?" asked Corey.

"Today it's on sale to you for $10.00," answered Mr. Wilbur, as he smiled with his huge moray eel teeth.

That Friday at school, Miss Mermaid brought out a tray of cupcakes.

Everyone sang "Happy Birthday" to Melissa.

"Thank you, Miss Mermaid!" shouted Melissa.

Melissa was so surprised and so happy!

After everyone ate, Corey and Tommy brought out a present for Melissa.
Tied to the bow was a big sand shovel.
"Wow! For me?" Melissa asked.

Melissa had a huge smile on her face as she started to tear off the wrapping paper.
"Melissa, shouldn't you open the card first?" asked Miss Mermaid.
"Oh, yeah," giggled Melissa.

Melissa opened the card, which was signed by all the sea kids, and read the words, "Happy Birthday, Melissa! We love you!"

Tears were running down Melissa's cheeks. "Thank you so much!" she shouted. The box was filled with colorful fabrics, ribbons, buttons, and trinkets. Melissa said, "I'll be able to make lots of things with all this great stuff."

The next day, Melissa came to school with handmade thank-you cards for her friends. Each card had a smile and a heart on it.

Melissa gave Corey a special card and said, "I'm sorry I bragged. I promise never to do that again. You're better than all the toys in the world, even better than a Snappy Cat Starfish lunchbox!"

Corey gave Melissa a big hug!

That night Melissa said a prayer to Jesus, "Dear Jesus, thank you for my mommy, daddy and my whole family, and thank you for all my wonderful friends at school who love me just like you do. Amen."

Melissa never bragged again. She was thankful for all her wonderful friends; they were better than all the toys in the sea!

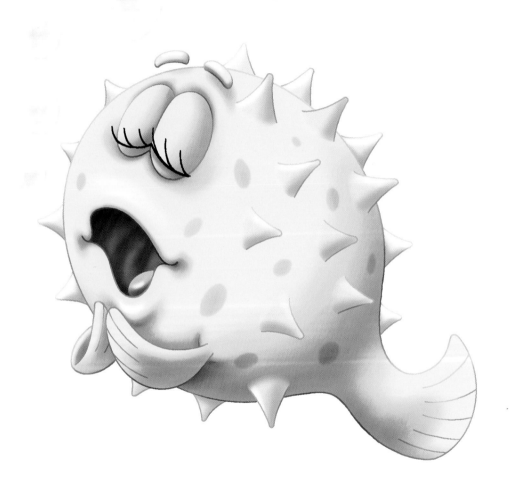

Remember, kids, to say your prayers and always have Jesus in your heart.
Have fun looking for the ⋉ hidden in the pictures!